9.90

ACTION SCIENCE

THE SEASHORE

Joyce Pope

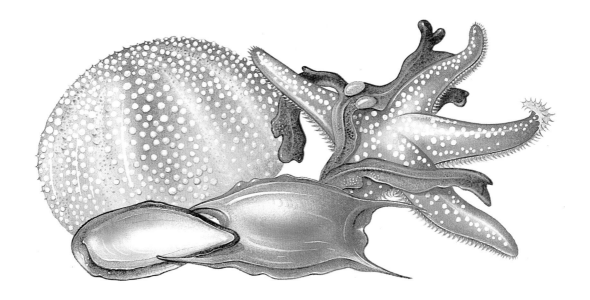

Franklin Watts

London New York Toronto Sydney

© 1985 Franklin Watts Ltd

First published in Great
Britain in 1985
by Franklin Watts Ltd
12a Golden Square
London W1

First published in the United
States of America by
Franklin Watts Inc.
387 Park Avenue South
New York
N.Y. 10016

Phototypeset by Tradespools
Ltd, Frome, Somerset
Printed in Italy

UK edition:
ISBN 0 86313 221 9
US edition:
ISBN 0-531-04951-5
Library of Congress
Catalog Card Number:
84-52005

Designed by
Ben White

Illustrated by
Colin Newman, Val Sangster/
Linden Artists,
and Chris Forsey

THE SEASHORE

ACTION SCIENCE

Contents

Equipment

As well as a few everyday items, you will need the following equipment to carry out the activities in this book.

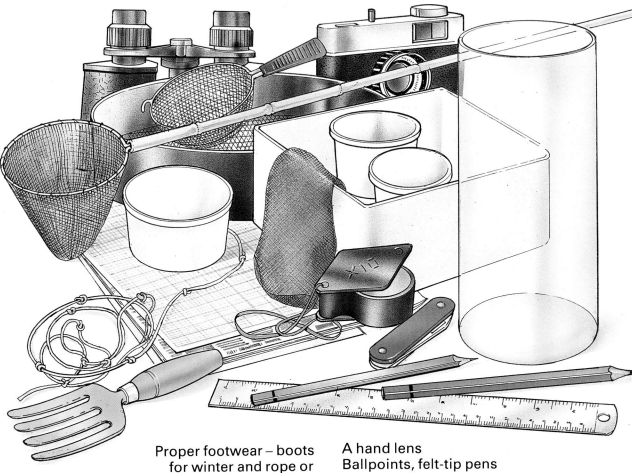

Proper footwear – boots
 for winter and rope or
 rubber soled shoes
 for summer
Suntan lotion
Plastic boxes
A lightweight fork
Plastic tubes
Plastic bags
A tape measure
A ball of thick string
A strong penknife

A hand lens
Ballpoints, felt-tip pens
 or pencils
Graph paper
Stiff white paper
Newspaper
A large bait seine
A nylon sieve
A ruler
A thermometer
Camera (if possible)
Binoculars

Introduction

The seashore is one of the most exciting places in the world to explore, but it can also be one of the most dangerous. If you follow these rules you should come to no harm.

1. Know the times of the tides. If you forget that the tide changes you might get cut off at high tide, which could be very dangerous. You also need to know the time of low tide if you are going to look at seashore plants and animals.

2. Always wear something on your feet, preferably with non-slip soles.

3. Listen to the weather forecast and wear the right clothes to protect you.

4. Listen to the advice of the Coast Guard or anybody else who knows the shore well. They may be able to warn you of local hazards.

5. Be careful especially after rough weather. Big waves may still come in unexpectedly, and could knock you off your feet.

6. Beware of sea cliffs. Don't sit under them because there could be falling rock. Never try to climb a sea cliff.

7. Always tell somebody where you are going.

8. Take some food and a drink with you.

9. If you have turned over stones or weed, always put them back.

10. Only collect those animals you specially want to watch and gently return them afterwards.

What is the seashore?

The seashore is the name given to the narrow area which is the junction between the land and the sea. Sometimes it is covered with water and is, in effect, part of the ocean. At other times, the water disappears and it becomes an extension of the land. The plants and animals that live there are different from those of the open sea and they can't live if brought on to dry land or put into fresh water.

The movements of the sea up and down the beach are called the tides. Tides are caused by the moon and sun, both of which pull the earth toward themselves by their force of gravity. The solid ground cannot move, but great areas of water, like the oceans, can be heaped up into tidal waves. Tides are often helped by the wind, which may drive the water further ashore, or hold it back.

▽ The tide is high twice in each 24 hours and rises a different amount each day. You can generally tell the height of the highest tide, for land plants will not grow in places that are regularly covered in salt water.

sandy shore

high tide line

Different kinds of seashore

The seashore may be cliffed and rocky, or flat and sandy – no two beaches are exactly the same. Where the land is mountainous or rugged, the seashore will form rocky headlands and little sandy coves. In lowland areas the seashore will be wide and flat and may be made of sand or pebbles.

Where a river runs into the sea, salt marshes occur. Salt marshes are different from all other kinds of beaches, because they are usually made of thick black mud, which is the home of many kinds of plants related to the flowering plants of the land. But, whichever type of seashore you may visit, you will always find lots of interesting plants and animals to investigate.

▽ The beach varies in width from wide sandy shores to narrow rocky areas. At low tide it is possible to see how far the water will rise, for the waves carry all kinds of debris and dump it at the highest point that they reach. This line of waste from the sea is called the high tide line.

rocky shore

A place to live

One of the first things that you discover about the sea is that it is salty. You might think that this would mean that the water would not be fit to drink. But the plants that live in it are able to use the salt directly for their growth.

The sea is never still, and it might seem that a storm, causing great waves to crash on to a beach, must be an enemy to all living things. But animals can shelter safely in the holes and crevices formed in hard rocks by the pounding waves. The splashing water contains oxygen, which all of the beach creatures need to breathe.

The sea is dense so it supports the heavy shells of animals like periwinkles or whelks which are armored against its battering force.

△ Most seashore plants are seaweeds, but a few flowering plants can grow by the shore.

Eelgrass grows under water and the flowers are even pollinated by the sea. Glasswort and sea lavender grow on salt marshes and marram grass and yellow horn poppy on sand dunes.

◁ You can see how salty the sea is by letting sea water evaporate from a dish or a plate.

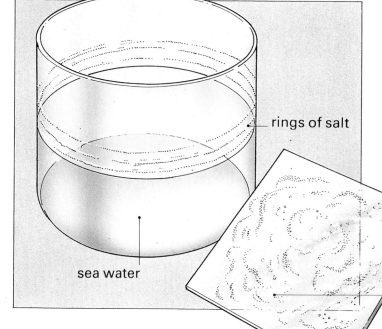

rings of salt

sea water

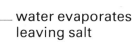

water evaporates leaving salt

△ The plants and animals of the shore are protected against the crashing waves which bring them oxygen and food.

△ The high tide line marks the highest point reached by the tide. Sometimes there is an extra line made by a storm.

△ The sea supports seaweeds and heavy bodied creatures such as crabs, which swim easily in the buoyant water.

Some effects of the tides

In addition to this, the sea supports the bodies of many tiny animals, too fragile to exist outside its protection. These include the young of most seashore creatures, which are swept to new homes by the movements of the waves.

When the tide is out, the wind and hot sun can raise the temperature of the beach. But this drops again the moment the incoming tide brings cold water from the open sea.

Seashore plants and animals have to be protected against the heat and dryness at low tide, but must also be able to survive when they are suddenly covered with cool water.

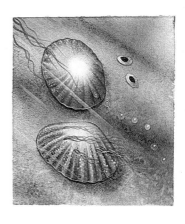

△ Limpets are not dislodged from the rocks by even the biggest waves. Each limpet hangs on tightly with a powerful, muscular foot.

9

Seashore zones

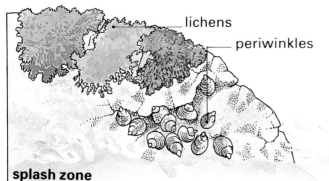

lichens

periwinkles

splash zone

▽ Each zone of the beach has different plants and animals. You can tell which zone you are on by checking with this diagram.

rough periwinkles

sea lettuce

channeled wrack

spiral wrack

Enteromorpha

upper beach

If you go down to the beach when the tide is almost high, you will be able to see that the water rises a little, but that it remains at its highest level for only a few minutes before it begins to fall.

This means that for much of the time, the animals and plants at the highest part of the beach are out of the water. The plants and animals near the bottom of the shore are uncovered only for a short time before the tide starts to come in again, so they spend most of their lives under water.

Animals and plants that live midway down the beach are submerged for half of their lives, and uncovered for the other half.

middle beach

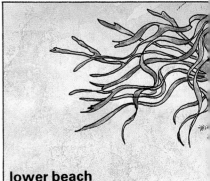

lower beach

sub-littoral zone

10

▷ Stretch a piece of string from a high point to a low point on the beach. Tie it to a rock and mark each end with a balloon, to check that you are keeping in a straight line. Note everything that your string touches. You can make a sort of line map of the beach on graph paper. This is called a transect.

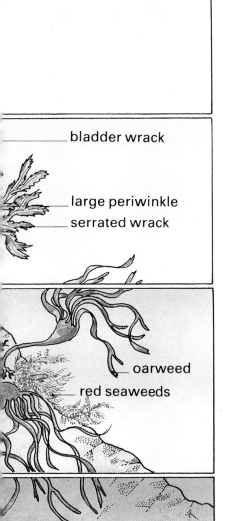

bladder wrack

large periwinkle
serrated wrack

oarweed
red seaweeds

The zones of the seashore

If you walk from the highest part of the shore to the lowest dry area at low tide, you will see that different sorts of plants and animals live on the high and low parts of the beach. This change in types of life is called zonation.

The beach can be divided into a series of strips, more or less parallel to the sea. Each strip has some plants and animals which differ from those in the strip above or below it.

Each of these zones has been given a name. The upper beach is only properly covered by the waters of the highest tides. Above it is the splash zone, which gets no more than wind-driven spray. Most of the middle beach is covered and uncovered every day, while the lower beach is only uncovered at times of the lowest tides. Below this area is the sub-littoral zone, which is never dry.

Sometimes, especially where there are deep rock pools, animals from a lower zone will be able to survive unexpectedly high up on the shore. At first you may not be certain which part of the beach you are on, but different types of seaweed are often good indicators of the various zones, as are the periwinkles.

11

Seaweeds

Many people think of seaweeds as being no more than a dangerous, slippery mat which covers the rocks at low tide, or a stinking mess of decaying rubbish on the high tide line.

You can only see the beauty of seaweeds when they are suported by the water, for they are not stiff enough to stand upright in the air. Yet they have a different sort of strength from land plants and many seaweeds can survive a battering from waves that would smash the toughest tree.

Seaweeds are slippery at low tide because they are covered with a jelly-like material which prevents them drying out in the sun and wind.

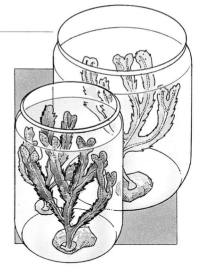

△ Put a piece of brown or red seaweed in a jar of sea water and you will see it float up, supported by the water. Put another piece in a jar of fresh water. It will begin to die and show green under the red or brown.

holdfast

12

Plants without flowers

Seaweeds are plants, yet they do not have roots, stems, leaves, flowers or fruit. Instead of roots, they cling to rocks and breakwaters by holdfasts, which often look like fingers. These holdfasts clutch the roughness of the stone.

Seaweeds are bathed in seawater, which gives them all the minerals they require for growth so they do not need stems or leaves with veins. They do not need flowers or fruit because new generations of seaweeds are formed from tiny male and female parts released directly into the water.

Seaweeds which live near the top of the rocky shore are often green-colored, like land plants. Those of the middle shore are usually sturdy brown plants, while those of the lower shore are generally fragile and a shade of red.

▽ Spread out some seaweed in a dish of salt water. Then slide a piece of stiff paper under it and arrange it. Lift the paper and seaweed out and put both on a thick layer of newspaper. Place a piece of nylon stocking over the seaweed and put more newspaper on top. Put a heavy weight on top to press everything flat. The seaweed will then stick itself to the paper.

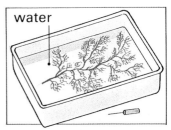

water

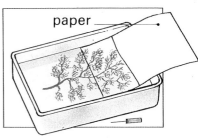

paper

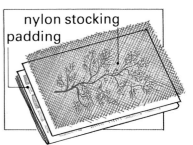

nylon stocking
padding

the seaweed will stick to the paper without glue

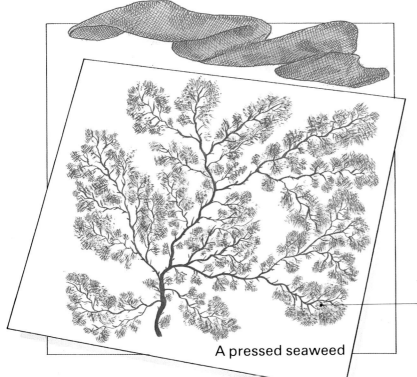

A pressed seaweed

13

Animals on the rocks

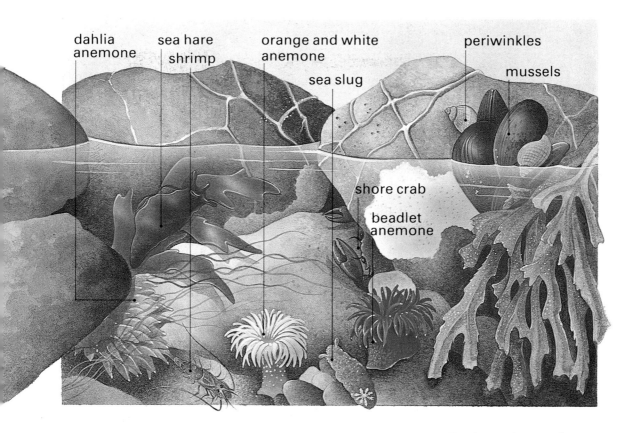

dahlia anemone
sea hare
shrimp
orange and white anemone
sea slug
periwinkles
mussels
shore crab
beadlet anemone

Rocky coastlines that have been worn away by the waves into pinnacles and pools give homes to the greatest variety of animals and plants. Some can find shelter in cracks and crevices, others, unable to stand drying out at low tide, may survive in rock pools, often the most colorful and interesting parts of the beach.

Animals that live on exposed rocks have to be able to withstand the force of storm waves. Acorn barnacles, when they are ready to start their adult life, glue themselves to the rock and grow a conical shell to protect their bodies.

△ Rock pools are often the most interesting parts of the shore, for they may contain plants and animals that are usually too far down the beach to be seen. In this rock pool there are seaweeds, anemones, barnacles, shore crabs, hermit crabs, and mussels.

14

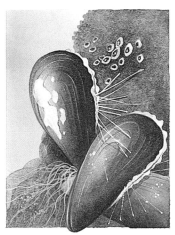

△ When the tide comes in mussels open their shells so that they can pump in sea water from which they filter their food.

acorn barnacles

△ At high tide barnacles open their shells and kick out what look like hairy feet which grab food and oxygen from the water.

Different ways of survival

Limpets, which are really cone-shaped snails, clamp themselves down by means of a large, muscular foot. Mussels attach themselves to the rocks by a group of threads called a byssus. Sea anemones are fixed by the base of their body column.

If need be, these animals can move about, but they are very slow and usually stay in one place. Some snails such as top shells and dog whelks have thick, heavy shells, so that they are not harmed if they are rolled about by the waves.

The seaweeds clinging to rocks often give protection to large numbers of small animals including many kinds of shrimps.

Crabs may also be found in rock pools when the tide is low. Hermit crabs, which are not completely armored, protect their soft abdomens in the shells of dead sea snails. Starfish die from exposure to the air, so they cling with their sucker-ended tube feet to the walls or bases of rock pools.

limpets

△ A limpet may travel and feed up to about 8 in (20cm) from its home spot but it must return there as the tide begins to fall.

△ Once they are covered by water, limpets move from their home spot to graze tiny seaweeds from the rocks.

Sea anemones are found on almost every rocky shore and even attach themselves to breakwaters and piers. They are completely soft-bodied animals whose name makes them sound like flowers.

They are circular in shape, but what look like petals are really tentacles armed with poisonous stings, ready to paralyze their prey. Stings from anemones that live in cool waters are not strong enough to hurt your hands, but those that live in warmer areas may well do so.

If a small fish or shrimp touches one of the anemone's tentacles, the sting cells shoot out huge numbers of poisonous threads. These quickly immobilize the prey, which is then pulled into the anemone's mouth.

▽ Sea anemones have poisonous sting cells. Curled up inside them are hollow threads with barbed ends. These are so fine that they cannot be seen without a microscope.

When something touches a trigger outside the cell the threads shoot out.

trigger

poison-filled harpoon

sea vase

dahlia anemone

hydroids
sea squirt

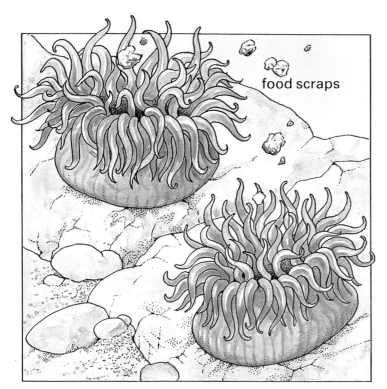

food scraps

△ Anemones cannot see, but they have a sense of smell and taste which enables them to recognize food (such as a piece of cheese that you may give them) or the small animal that may brush against them. Their prey is paralyzed in seconds and swallowed whole.

Ways of feeding

It is easy to test what an anemone will eat. Offer one a bit of ham or cheese and time how long it takes to accept or reject the food. Then try giving it a piece of crust. You could offer all sorts of foods to find out what an anemone will or will not eat.

There are lots of other flower-like animals on the rocks. One is called the golden star sea squirt. Each "petal" is really a separate living animal and so each "flower" is a group of them living together.

They take sea water in through their mouths, straining out and eating any tiny creatures that might be there and, at the same time, take oxygen from the water to breathe. This is called filter feeding. Many creatures of the sea and beach get their food this way. Even some quite large animals, such as the sea vase sea squirt, are filter feeders.

17

Animals under stones

Boulders on rocky or sandy beaches may shelter and protect lots of different sorts of creatures. Chitons (or coat-of-mail shells) often hide beneath overhangs of rock. Like limpets they move on big, muscular feet as they browse tiny seaweeds.

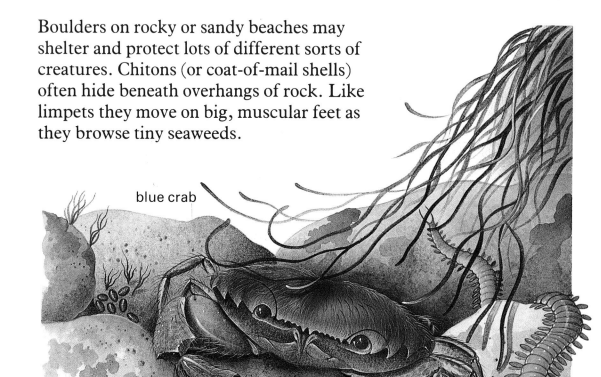

blue crab

clam worm

△ If you look under stones in rock pools you may find crabs or clam worms. Besides these there may be lots of small, fragile creatures which are worth a closer look.

Underneath stones in rock pools on the lower part of the shore you may find many kinds of brightly colored worms. The most noticeable are big clam worms, which may be over 8 in (20cm) long.

These animals move quickly, wriggling their bodies and beating the water with leg-like paddles. If you want to examine one closely, be careful how you handle it, as clam worms are hunters and if frightened can defend themselves with sharp, hooked jaws.

Crabs may shelter under rocks. Some are quick to defend themselves with their large claws, although others are more placid.

Crabs and their shells

If you want to look at one it is best to tempt it from its hiding place with a bit of meat or chicken bone on a string. The crab will grasp the tidbit and can usually be lifted clear of the water before it lets go.

Crabs and their relatives such as shrimps are at great risk from their enemies when they are shedding their shells. They have to do this in order to grow and they molt their old armor when it is outgrown.

Molting is controlled by hormones; when there are enough of these chemical messengers in a crab's blood, the shell splits and the crab wriggles out. Underneath there is a soft skin which can stretch for a time before it hardens to become a new body armor. Small crabs have to molt more often than big ones. You can very often find the cast shells of young crabs and other creatures on the shore or in rock pools.

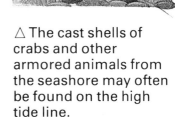

△ The cast shells of crabs and other armored animals from the seashore may often be found on the high tide line.

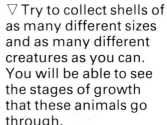

▽ Try to collect shells of as many different sizes and as many different creatures as you can. You will be able to see the stages of growth that these animals go through.

A collection of cast shore crab shells

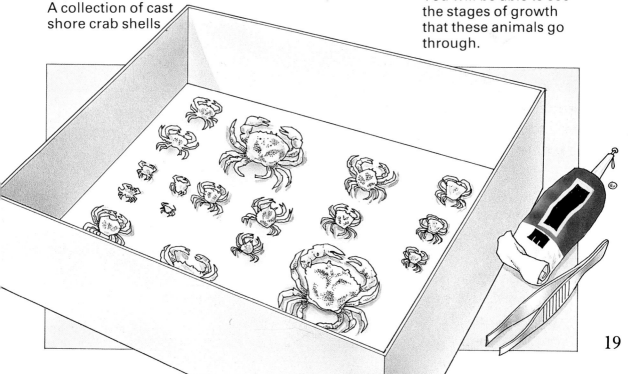

Burrows and tubes

Many shore creatures protect themselves by making tubes or burrows in which they can hide. The chief of these are worms, some of which make tubes of hard material.

These can often be seen on rocks high up on the shore or even covering the shells of big sea snails. They may look dead, for the animals inside do not show themselves unless they are quite certain that there is no danger.

If you put a stone or shell with tubes on it into a small tank of sea water and leave it for a while, the worms will push out a fan of fine tentacles with which they breathe as well as feed. The slightest jarring of the tank will instantly send the tentacles back into protective tubes.

△ A sandy shore may look empty, but there are often huge numbers of animals hidden in burrows beneath its surface.

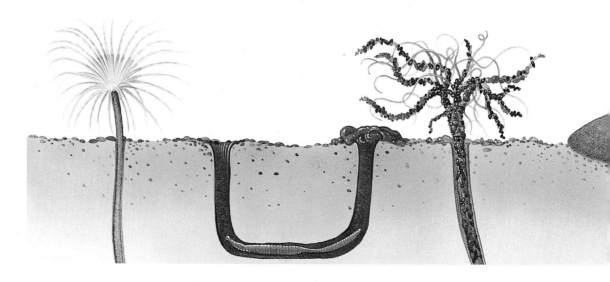

△ The fan worm is one of the largest of all tube worms. Its tube may be more than 8 in (20cm) long.

△ The lugworm is commonly found on sandy shores, where it lives in a U-shaped burrow.

△ It is often easy to see the tube of the sand builder on the beach, but the animal is usually well hidden.

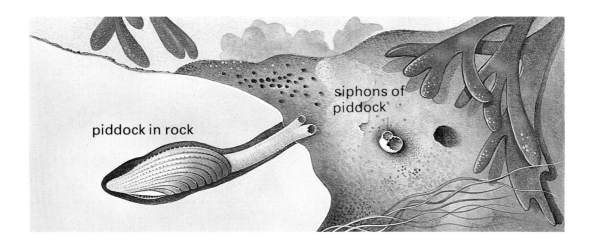

piddock in rock

siphons of piddock

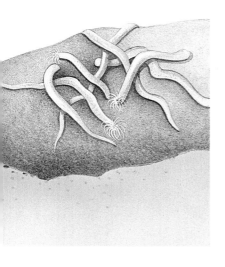

△ Piddocks are able to grind their way into soft rocks because their shells rasp holes which may be as much as 1 ft (30cm) deep. The outer end of the hole is small and may give no idea of the size of the animal inside.

△ The tubes of worms that protect themselves in calcareous coverings are found on most beaches.

Worms and shells in burrows

Some worms, such as the sand builder make long, deep burrows lined with sand grains cemented together. These stick up a little above the level of the beach. So do the shabby homes of the fan worms which are made of hardened mucus and fine sand grains. This is all that can usually be seen of these worms which are among the most beautiful of all of the shore creatures.

When conditions are quiet, these dull tubes flower into a crown of brilliantly colored tentacles which comb the water for oxygen and for food. If you find a fan worm, look closely and you will see dark spots on the tentacles. These are simple eyes that allow the worm to detect any movement which might mean danger. The worm spirals back into its tube, however slight the risk, like an umbrella folding.

A few kinds of animals can burrow into wood or soft rocks. The piddock bores into limestone which may be honeycombed with its short tunnels. From these, it pushes siphons into the sea to draw in water, for like many burrow makers, it is a filter feeder.

Below the sand

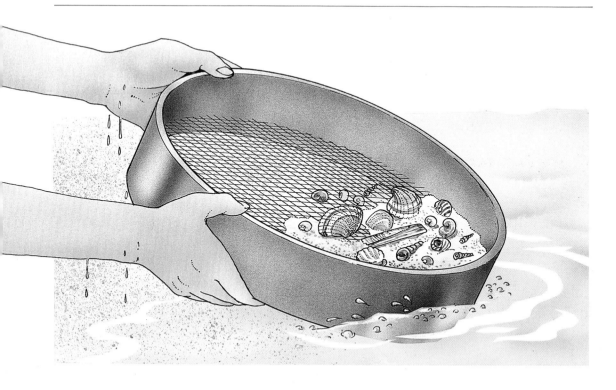

△ If you scoop some sand quickly into a sieve and swish it about in water, you may find some of the creatures that usually manage to escape when you dig for them.

After a storm, shells of many shapes may be washed out from under the sand.

Sandy or muddy beaches may look desolate and lifeless, but in fact there may be as many as 10,000 animals hidden at different depths beneath each square yard.

Some creatures, including shrimps and small flatfishes, lie on the surface of the sand. They are difficult to see, for they can change their color to match their background. Even sharp-eyed predators such as squids can only find them by stirring the sand to make them move.

Other animals bury themselves more deeply which is why most visitors to the seaside have no idea that the sands are so full of life. The main inhabitants of this environment are bivalve shells, such as cockles, venus shells and tellins.

Burrowers and their enemies

These expert diggers are all filter feeders and at high tide push two long tubes or siphons up to the surface of the sand. Sea water drawn in through one siphon is circulated round the body. Food and oxygen are removed and the water, plus waste products, and pumped out through the other siphon.

Different shells have siphons of varying lengths, so that they live like apartment dwellers, stacked one above the other.

Beach burrowers may become the prey of moon snails, which are predators that plow through the sand. When a moon snail comes upon a bivalve, it surrounds it with its large foot and rasps away with its tongue until a hole has been made in the shell. It continues to rasp, feeding on the living flesh of the helpless bivalve.

Dead shells neatly bored with a small hole may be found on many beaches and are evidence of the work of these hunters.

▽ Put some sand in a jar and cover it with sea water. Now put a living clam or other bivalve on to the sand and you will see it dig itself down and then push up its siphons to breathe.

siphons used for breathing and feeding

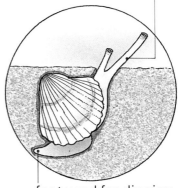

foot used for digging

scallop shell

wentletrap
razor shell

bivalve in sand

siphons of buried cockle

cockle shells

Seashore fishes

The fishes that we see in the market are almost all creatures of the open sea and are never found on the shore. The flounders are the chief exception to this, for not only do young flounders grow up on the beach, but also they often remain there, lying hidden in shallow, sandy pools, even when they are quite large.

Most beach fishes are small, rather dull colored creatures, so that they match the sand or gravel over which they live. They are mostly slow swimmers that feed on small, shrimplike creatures and other slow-moving animals.

▽ Many small fish live in rock pools on the beach. They are often difficult to see, because they are usually dull-colored creatures and they hide among the seaweed when the tide is low.

▷ Flatfish start life the same shape as other fishes, but as they grow they lie on one side and become flattened.

The eye on the underside of their body moves around until it is looking upward. Flatfish can change color to match the sand or gravel on which they are resting.

Beach fishes and their young

If the fishes are in danger they can wriggle into crevices or under rocks. During rough weather they may be battered by storms. Many beach fishes guard against this by having suckers, formed of two fins, on their undersides.

They hang on to rocks with these and are not washed away. Instead the sea breaks over their smooth, big-headed bodies without disturbing them.

Many beach fishes care for their young. Often it is the male who looks after the eggs. Seahorse and pipe fish females lay their eggs in a brood pouch on the underside of their mates who carry them until the baby fishes hatch a few weeks later.

In early summer male sticklebacks take up their own territories and build nests made from bits of weed. Each stickleback persuades several females to lay their eggs in the nest. The male then drives the females away and cares for the eggs and the baby fishes when they hatch.

25

Seashore birds

puffins

guillemots

Many sea birds are big, and almost all are black or gray and white in color. Most have webbed feet, and they are good swimmers. The easiest birds to see are the gulls who are scavengers and have discovered that there is always plenty to eat where human beings live.

They also hunt for small animals along the shore. Sometimes if you look in places where they have been resting, you may find pellets composed of indigestible parts of the gulls' food. This will enable you to see what they have been eating.

Gulls remain round the shore for the whole year, but many of the other sea birds come ashore for a short time during the summer months, when they nest and rear their young.

kittiwake

oystercatcher

Summer visitors

Terns, which look like small, fork-tailed
gulls, spend most of their life at sea, but often
nest in dense colonies on the beach. If you
know that terns are nesting, you should
always keep away from them, for they are
very easily disturbed and could abandon their
eggs or young as a result.

Another shore-nesting bird is the
oystercatcher. It uses its long bill to probe
into the sand to find cockles or other bivalves
on which it feeds.

Many sea birds nest on cliffs. You can see
kittiwakes' nests from a long way off, for their
white droppings stain the cliff face.

Guillemots and razorbills also lay their eggs
on ledges but they do not make any form of
nest for them. Puffins nest in holes in the
grassy slopes at the top of cliffs – sometimes
taking over rabbits' burrows.

▽ Most sea birds feed
on small fish or
invertebrates that they
catch in the sea. Bird
droppings fertilize the
water so that more life
can grow there.

Gulls often feed on
land or smash the shells
of clams on the rocks by
the sea.

gull with
broken bivalve

27

Beachcombing

One of the things that most people enjoy at the seaside is walking along the beach to see what they can find. There are many interesting objects that have been thrown up on to the shore or collected at the high tide line.

Shells are among the easiest things to find. Sometimes they may have been neatly bored by a moon snail. It is usually fairly easy to identify pieces of the shells of crabs, or the feathers of birds but many things swept up from the sea can be quite a puzzle. You may recognize a cuttlebone, which is the internal support of an animal related to the octopus. The bones of fishes, birds and sometimes mammals, bleached and rounded by the sea, are sometimes quite difficult to identify.

▽ Many of the objects that you may find on the beach are very fragile, so you will need to put them into boxes or tubes to protect them.

Wash the objects when you get home. This will remove salt and help to stop them from smelling.

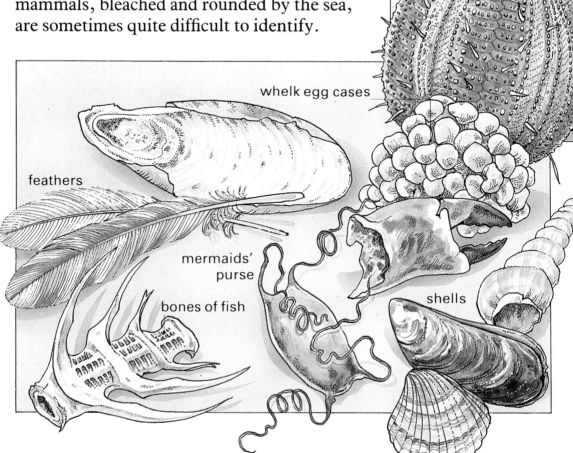

sea urchin shell

whelk egg cases

feathers

mermaids' purse

bones of fish

shells

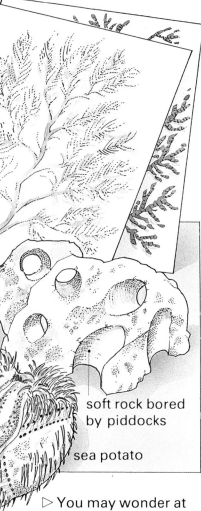

pressed seaweeds

soft rock bored
by piddocks

sea potato

Puzzles on the beach

Egg cases of many sorts are common among beach debris. Mermaids' purses are the egg cases of various dogfishes and skates. Each purse contained one large, yolky egg. The stringy looking object often found on the beach is the egg case of a channeled whelk. You could try and count how many eggs the case held.

The shells of sea urchins are sometimes washed up. Usually these lose their spines soon after the animal dies, but you may find one which still contains its curious teeth. These are called an Aristotle's Lantern, because the whole structure looks like an old fashioned light.

Teeth of fishes are sometimes found. The most puzzling are from the back of the throat of a shore fish called the wrasse. They are known as phryangeal teeth.

And just to remind you that the seashore is one of the most ancient of environments, you can often find fossils there, that can be added to your interesting collection of things from the seashore.

▷ You may wonder at the shapes of some of the things that you find on the beach. They may have grown in this way so that the plants or animals could reach light or food. Some dead plants or animals have been eroded into strange shapes.

When the outer shell of the sea snail is worn away you can see the central support shaped like a spiral staircase.

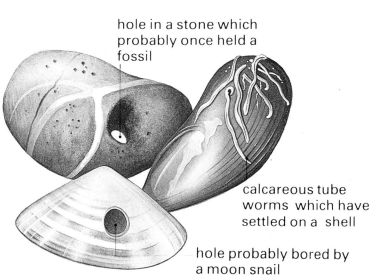

hole in a stone which probably once held a fossil

calcareous tube worms which have settled on a shell

hole probably bored by a moon snail

29

Glossary

Alga (plural algae)
The scientific name for seaweed and some very small related plants which are found in the sea and fresh water.

Aristotle's Lantern
The 5-toothed feeding apparatus of sea urchins. It is named after Aristotle, an ancient Greek naturalist, who first described it.

Bivalve
A creature such as a clam, a cockle or an oyster, whose soft body is protected in a two-part, hinged shell.

Erosion
The wearing away of hard substances by natural forces such as the wind or the sea. The sea erodes large things like cliffs, breaking them down into pebbles and sand. Small things like shells are eventually destroyed.

Filter feeding
Feeding on very tiny living things which float in sea water, by straining them in some way from the water. Many kinds of seashore creatures feed in this way.

The tides
Something about the tides which may be puzzling to you is the fact that at some times the water comes much further up the beach and goes much further back toward the sea than it does at others.

This is because although the moon is the main force in pulling up the tides, the sun helps as well. Since sun, moon and earth are all moving, at some times the sun and moon will be pulling together.

This happens just after new and full moon, when the tides are highest. They are called spring tides – whatever the time of the year.

At about the time of half moon each month, the sun and moon are pulling against each other. At these times neap tides occur which uncover little of the shore. If you want to study the seashore, make certain that you visit it at spring tides. A calendar will probably tell you the days when the moon is new or full.

Remember too, that the time of the tides changes, becoming a little later each day. It is best to arrive at the beach as the water is falling and to follow the tide down. You will then see freshly uncovered plants and animals.

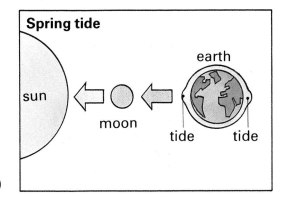

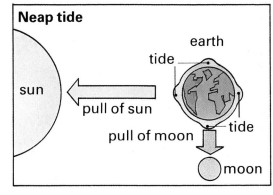

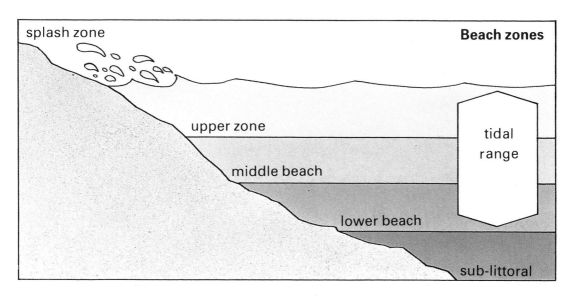

Beach zones

splash zone

upper zone

middle beach

lower beach

sub-littoral

tidal range

Fossils
The remains of plants or animals of the past which have been preserved in rock. The seashore is a good place to look for fossils, since the waves often erode them from the cliffs, and they then fall on to the shore.

Hormone
A chemical produced by glands in an animal's body. Hormones act as messengers to tell the body to do special things, like growing or molting.

Invertebrate
An animal without a backbone. Most animals like worms, insects or sea anemones are invertebrates.

Molt
The process of shedding hair, feathers or skin, usually in the course of growth.

Neap tides
The name given to tides at about the time of half moon each month. Neap tides do not come far up the beach, nor is the lower shore exposed at low tide.

Oxygen
A gas which forms about 20% of the air. Plants give it off as a waste product of their growth but all animals need it to breathe.

Pellet
A sausage-shaped lump, produced by birds, composed of indigestible material such as hair, bones or pieces of shell. By examining the remains of foodstuff in a pellet, it is possible to find out what a bird has been eating.

Siphon
A tube which is part of the body of various sea snails and bivalves. Filter feeders use siphons to take in water to feed. Wastes are pumped out through a second siphon.

Spring tides
The very high tides that occur at about the times of new and full moon each month throughout the year. At these times the lower beach is fully exposed.

Index